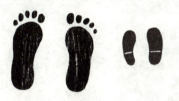

BIG FOOT
and LITTLE FOOT

AMULET BOOKS • NEW YORK

BOOK 5

THE GREMLIN'S SHOES

Story by Ellen Potter

Art by Felicita Sala

For Erica Finkel, who helped me find my way
through the cold North Woods

PUBLISHER'S NOTE: This is a work of fiction. Names, characters, places, and incidents are either the product of the author's imagination or used fictitiously, and any resemblance to actual persons, living or dead, business establishments, events, or locales is entirely coincidental.

Library of Congress Cataloging-in-Publication Data
Names: Potter, Ellen, 1963- author. | Sala, Felicita, illustrator.
Title: The gremlin's shoes / story by Ellen Potter ; art by Felicita Sala.
Description: New York : Amulet Books, 2021. | Series: Big Foot and Little Foot ; book 5 | Audience: Ages 6 to 9. | Summary: Determined to buy a Marvelous Monster Magnet, Hugo and Boone set out to earn the money on an adventure through the woods, where they meet some interesting new friends.
Identifiers: LCCN 2020035800 | ISBN 9781419743245 (hardcover) | ISBN 9781419743252 (paperback) | ISBN 9781683357926 (ebook)
Subjects: CYAC: Sasquatch–Fiction. | Friendship–Fiction. | Moneymaking projects–Fiction. | Adventure and adventurers–Fiction. | Monsters–Fiction.
Classification: LCC PZ7.P8518 Gre 2021 | DDC [E]–dc23
LC record available at https://lccn.loc.gov/2020035800

Text © 2021 Ellen Potter
Illustrations © 2021 Felicita Sala
Book design by Brenda E. Angelilli

Printed and bound in U.S.A.
10 9 8 7 6 5 4 3 2 1

Amulet Books are available at special discounts when purchased in quantity for premiums and promotions as well as fundraising or educational use. Special editions can also be created to specification. For details, contact specialsales@abramsbooks.com or the address below.

Amulet Books® is a registered trademark of Harry N. Abrams, Inc.

ABRAMS The Art of Books
195 Broadway, New York, NY 10007
abramsbooks.com

The Big Foot and Little Foot series

1

Nothing-to-do-itis

Deep in the cold North Woods, there lived a young Sasquatch named Hugo. He was bigger than you but smaller than me, and he was hairier than both of us. He lived in apartment 1G in the very back of Widdershins Cavern with his mother and father and his older sister, Winnie.

It was Saturday, so there was no school. Hugo and his best friend, Boone, sat on the floor of Hugo's bedroom, dipping their fingers into the little stream that ran through the room. Tiny silver fish swam in the stream. Boone and Hugo made their hands into tunnels for the fish to swim through.

"So, what do you want to do today?" Boone asked Hugo for the fifth time that morning.

"I don't know. What do you want to do today?" Hugo replied, also for the fifth time.

"I don't know," said Boone.

Hugo and Boone had a bad case of Nothing-to-do-itis. You've probably had

Nothing-to-do-itis once or twice in your life, too. It's when you suddenly have loads of free time, but you can't think of a single thing to do with it.

"Are those new shoes?" Hugo asked Boone.

Boone nodded and looked proudly at his red sneakers with black stripes and yellow laces. "The old ones were getting too small."

Hugo didn't have to wear shoes. Sasquatches have tough padding on the soles of their feet so they can walk barefoot. Still, Hugo thought it might be fun to wear red sneakers with black stripes and yellow laces.

Right then, he made a mental list of Reasons Why It Would Be Fun to Be a Human. "Sneakers" was number one on the list.

"Grandma told me that if my feet keep growing so fast," Boone said, "they'll be as big as a Sasquatch's in no time."

He placed his foot next to Hugo's foot to compare. Boone's foot was only half as big as Hugo's. But because Hugo didn't want to discourage Boone, he replied, "Bigger, maybe."

They were quiet for a moment. Then Boone asked for the sixth time, "So, what do you want to do today?"

Hugo was about to reply "I don't know" again when suddenly, he did have an idea.

"We could go to Uncle Figgy's Toy Store," he suggested.

"Yes! That's exactly what we should do!" Boone said, jumping to his feet.

And just like that, their case of Nothing-to-do-itis was cured.

2

Uncle Figgy's Toy Store

They headed out the door and down the winding passageways to Uncle Figgy's Toy Store. Like all the other shops in Widdershins Cavern, it was in the busy Central Cave District.

Hugo and Boone walked past the barbershop first. Sasquatch hair grows very fast, so there were always lots of Sasquatches in the barbershop waiting for a trim. Some of them wanted fancy hairdos, too. Today, Hugo and Boone spotted Mrs. Rattlebags sitting in a chair and having all her hair put in curlers.

Next they passed the Everything-You-Need General Store and Bakery. That was the store Hugo's parents owned. Hugo and Boone waved at Hugo's dad, who was behind the checkout counter, and he smiled and waved back.

Up ahead was Uncle Figgy's Toy Store. The toy store was always a popular place to be on Saturday, but today it was packed with squidges (which is what you call young Sasquatches).

"The store must have gotten some really great new toy," Hugo said.

"Look, there's Gigi." Boone pointed to a small squidge with glasses who was standing outside the toy store.

"Gigi!" Hugo and Boone called to her.

Gigi turned around and, looking a little embarrassed, waited for them to come over.

"What's happening?" asked Hugo.

"*That's* happening," Gigi said, pointing to a sign outside the store.

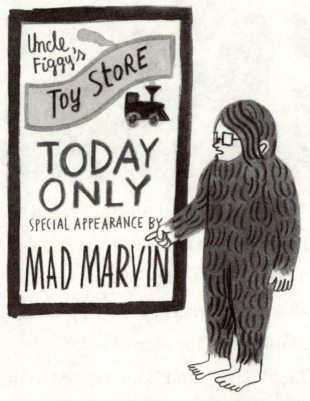

"Mad Marvin!" Hugo and Boone cried at the same time.

Mad Marvin was a celebrity! All the squidges in the cavern collected Mad Marvin's Monster Cards. They were trading cards that featured different monsters, like Fuzzy Ogres and Giant Armored Worms. Hugo had collected one hundred packs of them.

"I don't know why everyone is making such a fuss," Gigi said. "He's just a Sasquatch like any other Sasquatch."

"Then why are *you* here?" Hugo asked her.

"Oh, I'm just . . . um . . . I'm . . ." She sighed. "Okay, I'm curious to see what he looks like."

Hugo, Boone, and Gigi squeezed into Uncle Figgy's Toy Store along with lots of other excited squidges and some grown-up Sasquatches. Two of their classmates, Pip and Malcolm, were near the counter where Uncle Figgy stood. (Uncle Figgy wasn't actually anyone's uncle, by the way. Everyone just called him Uncle Figgy.)

"Can I have your attention, please?" Uncle Figgy cried in an excited voice. "Today, Uncle Figgy's Toy Store is honored to receive a visit from the incredible, the amazing, the legendary . . . *Mad Marvin!*"

The door behind Uncle Figgy opened.

Everyone in the store fell silent. Then a tall, thin Sasquatch with spiky electric-blue hair stepped out.

3

Mad Marvin

Hellooooo!" said Mad Marvin, waving his arms and hopping up and down. He had a lot of energy. "Who here believes in monsters?"

A bunch of squidges raised their hands, including Hugo and Boone. Gigi half raised her hand. "Excellent! Because this month, I've been touring caverns all over

the country to share a special announcement—"

Suddenly, Mad Marvin stopped talking
and frowned. He lifted his nose in the air
and sniffed. Sasquatches have an excel-

lent sense of smell, and it looked like Mad Marvin was smelling something he didn't like.

"Okay, everyone, don't panic!" Mad Marvin said, which of course made everyone start to panic and look around nervously.

"Maybe Mad Marvin brought a real live monster with him!" one squidge cried, and that made everyone panic even more. It seemed like any minute, there might be a stampede of terrified Sasquatches.

"Stay calm, stay calm!" Mad Marvin pleaded. "My nose might be wrong, but . . ." He took another long sniff. "I think I smell a HUMAN!"

There was a sigh of relief from the crowd.

"Aw, that's just Boone," one of the little squidges said. "He goes to our school."

The crowd parted so that Mad Marvin could see Boone. Boone was so much shorter than all the Sasquatches that Mad Marvin hadn't spotted him.

Boone grinned shyly and waved.

Mad Marvin looked astonished. "Well, I've seen a Slime-Tongued Werecat and a Lumpen Murch, but in all my travels, I've never seen a Human who was friends with Sasquatches!"

Everyone patted Boone's back and tweaked his ears fondly. They all liked Boone, and now they were proud that they had shocked the famous Mad Marvin!

"As I was saying," continued Mad Marvin, "I have a special announcement to make. I have a brand-new invention for all my monster-loving fans. Would you like to see it?"

"Yes!" some squidges called out.

"I *said* . . . WOULD YOU LIKE TO SEE IT?!" Mad Marvin repeated more loudly.

"YES!!!" the crowd shouted back.

"Okay . . . *BLAMMO!*" Mad Marvin snapped his fingers, and a thick cloud of green smoke appeared. Hugo and Boone gasped. For a moment, no one could see Mad Marvin.

"That's just a simple Smoke Snapper," Gigi said. "You can buy them in any old prank shop."

Gigi was kind of ruining the fun, Hugo thought.

When the smoke cleared, Mad Marvin was holding something in his hand.

"Presenting . . . MAD MARVIN'S MAR-VELOUS MONSTER MAGNET!" he cried.

4

The Marvelous Monster Magnet

The Marvelous Monster Magnet was just a disc of wood with little holes around its border. It didn't look especially marvelous.

"It's just a round piece of wood," Malcolm said.

"WRONG, young squidge!" said Mad Marvin, jabbing a finger at Malcolm.

"Then what does it do, Mad Marvin?" Pip called out.

"I'm glad you asked!" said Mad Marvin. "The Marvelous Monster Magnet lets you meet monsters, up close and personal!"

Gigi snorted in disbelief.

"Isn't that dangerous?" asked Pip.

"Not all monsters are dangerous," replied Mad Marvin. "In fact, I've heard that Humans think Sasquatches are monsters. Isn't that right, Boone?"

Everyone in the store looked at Boone, who turned bright red and nodded. He was embarrassed to admit that most Humans *did* think Sasquatches were monsters.

"Would you like to see how the

Marvelous Monster Magnet works?" Mad Marvin asked.

"YES!!" the crowd called out.

"Or *doesn't* work," muttered Gigi.

"*Shhh*," Hugo told her.

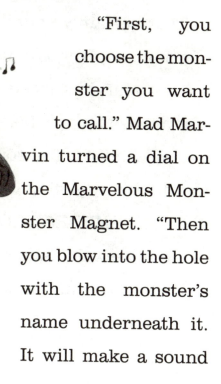

"First, you choose the monster you want to call." Mad Marvin turned a dial on the Marvelous Monster Magnet. "Then you blow into the hole with the monster's name underneath it. It will make a sound that the monster won't be able to resist. If that monster is lurking in the area, it will come right to you. Now, let's see . . ." He examined the Marvelous Monster Magnet. "Let's call a Sticky-Toed Grub Growler."

That certainly sounded like a dangerous monster, Hugo thought.

Mad Marvin turned the dial, put the Marvelous Monster Magnet to his mouth, and blew into it. The sound that came out was a deep, rumbling growl.

"GRRRRRRRROOOO!"

"Now we wait," said Mad Marvin.

Everyone was perfectly silent, eyes wide, waiting for the Sticky-Toed Grub Growler.

They waited for one minute. Then another. Then another.

Nothing happened.

Gigi leaned over to Hugo and whispered, "Told you."

That's when they heard a *phloop-phlooop-phloop* sound. Everyone looked around to see where it was coming from.

Phloop-phlooop-phloop!

"Up there!" One of the squidges pointed at the ceiling.

Everyone looked up.

Walking above their heads, its hairless pink feet sticking to the ceiling, was a small creature with silver scales on its back and a long, pointed snout. It waddled

along, its feet making that *phloop-phloop* sound each time they lifted off the ceiling.

Mad Marvin blew into the Marvelous Monster Magnet again.

"GRRRRRRRROOOO!"

The creature responded, *"GRRRRRRR-ROOOO! GRRRRRRRROOOO!"*

Then it made one loud *PHLOOOP!* sound and launched itself off the ceiling, tumbled through the air, and landed directly on Mad Marvin's shoulder.

5

Twenty-Five Nubbins

For a moment, no one said anything. They were too surprised. Even Gigi was gawping at the strange little creature perched on Mad Marvin's shoulder, its long snout twitching.

Then one of the squidges called out, "I want a Marvelous Monster Magnet!"

"Me too!" cried another.

"And me!"

Boone turned to Hugo. "We *have* to get one, Hugo!"

Hugo and Boone were going to become cryptozoologists when they grew up. ("Cryptozoologist" is a hard-to-say word for someone who studies mysterious creatures, which are called cryptids.) A Marvelous Monster Magnet would really come in handy for a cryptozoologist.

"Just think," said Hugo, "instead of searching all over for cryptids, we could simply blow into the Marvelous Monster Magnet, and the creatures would come to us!"

"We'd like one, too!" Boone called out to Mad Marvin.

Mad Marvin reached down beneath the checkout counter and held up a carton. "Luckily, I have brought a whole box of Marvelous Monster Magnets. Plus, I have personally signed each one."

"*Oooo!*" the crowd cried.

"How much are they?" Gigi asked, which was a very sensible question.

"Only twenty-five nubbins!" Mad Marvin said.

Gigi turned to Hugo and Boone. "Do either of you have twenty-five nubbins?" she asked.

Hugo's and Boone's smiles faded. They looked at each other worriedly. Twenty-five nubbins was a lot of money.

"I *had* two nubbins," Hugo said. "But I spent them on some Stink Sap. How many nubbins do you have, Boone?"

"I don't have *any* nubbins," Boone said. "Humans just have dollars and cents, and I don't have any of those, either."

For a moment, they lost all hope of buying a Marvelous Monster Magnet.

But then Hugo had an idea.

"We could earn the money," he suggested.

"We could!" Boone agreed. "I once made money by walking our neighbor's dog."

"But there are no dogs in Widdershins Cavern," Hugo said. "Sasquatches are afraid of dogs."

"Oh, right." Boone nodded, remembering how scared Hugo had been when he had met Boone's dog, Mogi.

"If you ask me, it looks like Uncle Figgy could use some help," said Gigi, gesturing to all the customers crowded around the counter.

"Good idea, Gigi," said Hugo.

Hugo and Boone headed up to the counter, where Uncle Figgy was frantically trying to help everyone at the cash register.

"Hey, no cutting the line!" one squidge yelled at Hugo and Boone.

"We're not cutting," said Hugo. "We just have to ask Uncle Figgy a question."

When they got to the counter, Uncle Figgy was putting a handful of wooden nubbins in the cash register. "Twenty-two, twenty-three, twenty-four, and twenty-five," he counted out. Then he handed a Marvelous Monster Magnet to a full-grown Sasquatch.

"Have fun with it!" Uncle Figgy told the Sasquatch.

"Oh . . . ahem . . . it's for my nephew," the Sasquatch muttered, but Hugo could tell it was really for him.

"You look very busy, Uncle Figgy," Boone said.

"Busiest day of the year!" Uncle Figgy said happily without even looking at Boone. He was too busy taking nubbins from his next customer.

"You could hire us to help you," said Hugo.

"We're very responsible," Boone added.

"Hmm." Uncle Figgy considered. "I do have a toy that needs to be delivered to a customer today. And it looks like I'm going to be so busy with these Marvelous Monster Magnets that I won't be able to get to the post office before it closes. Tell you what—see that box there?" He pointed to a small box behind the counter with an address written on it. "I'll pay you two nub-bins if you take it to the post office."

"Done!" Boone said.

"And tell Mr. Kipper that it needs to go express delivery."

"We will!" said Hugo.

Uncle Figgy took two nubbins out of his register and handed them to Boone.

"Just twenty-three more nubbins to go," said Hugo as he picked up the box.

6

Express Delivery

At the post office, there was another long line.

"I hope Uncle Figgy doesn't run out of Marvelous Monster Magnets before we can earn enough money," Hugo said anxiously as they waited for their turn.

"We'll have to get some more jobs around the cavern," said Boone.

"Maybe the barbershop could use help sweeping up all that hair."

Finally, they reached the front of the line, and Hugo placed the box on the counter.

"Hi, Mr. Kipper. Uncle Figgy says this needs to go express delivery."

Mr. Kipper looked at the label. "Going to Green Hollow Cave, huh? Well, I'm afraid this will have to go out on Monday. Our postal carrier is sick and can't make any deliveries today."

"You could hire Hugo and me to deliver the package," said Boone. "We're really dependable."

Mr. Kipper looked uncertain.

"We've already earned our Bimble Badges," Hugo told him.

A squidge with a Bimble Badge could go into the North Woods on their own whenever they liked.

"And we'd only charge you four nubbins," Boone added.

Hugo thought that sounded like too much money. He held his breath as Mr. Kipper considered it.

"That seems fair," Mr. Kipper finally said. "Green Hollow Cave is behind the

Silver Thread Waterfall on the west side of the woods."

"Oh, sure, I know that waterfall," Boone told him.

Mr. Kipper opened his cash register, took out four nubbins, and started to hand them to Hugo. But then he reconsidered and gave them to Boone instead.

"You'd better keep them, since you have pockets," he said.

Hugo added another item to his list of Reasons Why It Would Be Fun to Be a Human:

1. sneakers
2. pockets

7

Chupacabra Howl

Hugo made a quick stop at the Everything-You-Need General Store and Bakery to ask his parents if he could go to Green Hollow Cave with Boone.

"I guess it's okay," Hugo's mom said uncertainly. "Just be back home before dark."

Then she reminded them about all the

dangers in the woods, like poison ivy and tree roots that could sprain your ankles and, most importantly, Humans.

"Sorry, Boone, dear," she said, "but not all Humans are as nice to Sasquatches as you are."

Then she kissed them both good-bye, and they set off on their journey.

It had rained in the North Woods the night before. Now there was a smoky white fog that drifted between the trees, as though the clouds had come down from the sky to have a look around.

"I wonder if the Marvelous Monster Magnet can attract a chupacabra," Boone said.

Hugo had read about chupacabras in Boone's *The Biggest Ever Book of Cryptids*. The book said that a chupacabra was the size of a bear, had

spines down its back, and sucked blood from goats.

"Maybe that's the sort of monster we *don't* want to attract," Hugo suggested. "Let's look at those nubbins again." It wasn't often that he had six nubbins all at once.

Boone reached into his pocket, pulled out the nubbins, and handed them to Hugo. Hugo jiggled them in his hand so they made a nice *clunk*ing noise.

"I wonder what a chupacabra sounds like?" Boone said.

"Maybe it barks like a dog," Hugo suggested.

"Nah," Boone said. "Not scary enough."

A barking dog seemed very scary to Hugo, but he didn't say that.

"I think it would howl like this . . ." Boone lifted his head and cried out, "*AYIYIYIYIYI!*"

There was a rustle in the thick woods in front of them. A few leaves shivered as if something had brushed against them. There was another rustle, then a *snap-snap* of twigs.

Hugo and Boone stopped walking.

"There's something over there," Boone whispered.

Hugo lifted his nose in the air and sniffed.

"It smells strange," he whispered.

Boone sniffed the air. "All I can smell is air."

Hugo wondered what it would be like not to have an excellent sense of smell. There were good and bad parts about being a Human, he thought. The good parts were that you got to have sneakers and pockets. But a bad part was that your sniffer didn't work very well.

Hugo took another sniff. "It smells sort of like a Sasquatch . . ." He sniffed again. "But sort of not."

Hugo wondered if that was what a chupacabra smelled like.

From somewhere close by, they heard a snort.

"What was that?" Boone asked.

"I don't know."

The snort came again, louder this time. Suddenly, there was a thunderous *thump-thump-thump-thump* in the underbrush, and through the fog, Hugo and Boone caught sight of a massive beast heading straight toward them.

"Run!" Hugo shouted.

8

Rufus P. Winterberry

Hugo and Boone tore through the woods, turning this way and that, trying to escape the beast that was charging them. Whatever the thing was, it was fast. Each time they thought they'd dodged it, its thunderous footsteps started up again right behind them a few seconds later.

"Stop! *Stop!!*" someone yelled.

"Hugo, did you hear that?" Boone asked breathlessly as they ran.

"Stop!"

"I think someone needs help," said Hugo.

"STOP!!" The voice was so close now that Hugo and Boone stopped and turned around, only to see the beast hurtling straight at them. It was very tall with a droopy snout and two enormous antlers. Although Hugo had never actually seen one in the woods before, he knew exactly what the creature was.

A moose.

And riding on top of the moose was a Sasquatch wearing a large hat.

"*STOP, THIEF!*" the Sasquatch shouted as the moose came to a halt in front of Hugo and Boone.

"Where? Where? Where's the thief?" Boone asked, looking all around him.

"*You're* the thief!" The Sasquatch pointed at Boone.

"Me?" Boone cried.

"Yes, of course *you*, you lousy

squidge-stealing Human!" The Sasquatch hopped off the moose and towered over Boone menacingly. "Let the squidge go. NOW!"

"What squidge? You mean Hugo?" asked Boone.

"Don't play games with me, Human, or you will face the wrath of Rufus P. Winterberry!"

"Who's Rufus P. Winterberry?" Boone
asked.

"*I'm* Rufus P. Winterberry," the Sasquatch replied. He was an old Sasquatch
with gray patches of hair on his elbows
and knees, but he looked strong.

"I'm Boone," Boone said in a friendly

way. He held out his hand for Mr. Winterberry to shake.

This seemed to confuse the Sasquatch. He hesitated for a moment, then reluctantly shook Boone's hand. *"Hmmph.* You have good manners for a thief."

"He's *not* a thief!" said Hugo. "Boone is my best friend."

"Best friend?" Mr. Winterberry stared at them in surprise. "A Sasquatch and a Human?" He snorted. "Impossible! Who ever heard of such a thing?"

"Who ever heard of a Sasquatch riding a moose?" Hugo snapped.

In fact, Hugo thought riding a moose looked like fun. But he was annoyed with Mr. Winterberry for calling Boone a thief.

"A moose is the best way to travel," said Mr. Winterberry.

"I like boats better," Boone said.

"Have you ever ridden a moose?" Mr. Winterberry asked.

"Have you ever ridden in a boat?" Boone countered.

Mr. Winterberry sniffed. "A moose is better," he said decisively. "Aren't you, Sprinkles? Aren't you better than a boat?" He petted the moose's side affectionately. Sprinkles turned and looked at Mr. Winterberry adoringly with his large brown eyes and nuzzled his shoulder.

He really was a very well-behaved moose, Hugo thought. He reached out and patted Sprinkles.

It was then that Hugo realized something awful.

"Oh no!" he cried, staring
at his open hand.

"What's wrong?"
Boone asked.

"They're gone!"

"What's gone?"

"Our nubbins!"
Hugo wailed. "Our nubbins are gone!"

9

Hidden Treasure

Hugo thought through what must have happened. He had been holding the nubbins when the moose began to chase them. In all the confusion, he must have dropped them somewhere in the woods.

Hugo, Boone, and even Mr. Winterberry searched all over for the nubbins. They tried to retrace their steps. They checked in mud puddles and under bushes and piles of twigs. But in the end, they had to face the facts—the nubbins were gone for good.

"If only I had pockets," Hugo said mournfully, "this never would have happened."

"Cheer up," Mr. Winterberry said. "They're not the last nubbins you'll ever have."

"But we *needed* those nubbins," said Hugo. "We were saving up to buy a Marvelous Monster Magnet."

"Hmm. A Marvelous Monster Magnet? That sounds expensive," Mr. Winterberry said.

"It is. It costs twenty-five nubbins."

Mr. Winterberry thought for a moment. Then, in a low voice, he said, "Can you two keep a secret?"

Hugo and Boone nodded.

"I've traveled for three days to reach the North Woods because I'm on an important quest," Mr. Winterberry told them.

"What sort of important quest?" asked Boone.

"*Shhh!*" Mr. Winterberry looked around to make sure no one else was listening. "I'm looking for hidden treasure. A very *valuable* hidden treasure."

"Are you sure it's in the North Woods?" Hugo asked.

"Of course I'm sure." Mr. Winterberry

looked at them carefully. "I don't suppose you two know anyone I could hire to help me look for it?"

Boone perked right up. He folded his arms over his chest and raised his chin. In a very businesslike voice, he said, "I think we can help you, Mr. Winterberry! Hugo and I are experts at finding things."

"Are you?"

"Yes. In fact, we run the Big Foot and Little Foot Detective Agency."

Hugo glanced at Boone. He had never heard of the Big Foot and Little Foot Detective Agency before.

"Then it's a lucky thing I ran into you!" Mr. Winterberry said. "I would like to hire you both to find the treasure. If you find it, I'll split it with you. What do you say?"

"Yes!" Boone cried.

"Um, okay," Hugo said.

Mr. Winterberry reached up to his hat. Stuck in the hatband was a tattered piece of paper folded in half. He pulled it out and handed it to Boone. "This should help." Then Mr. Winterberry sat down beneath a

tree. "Good luck, detectives! Sprinkles and I will wait right here for you."

Mr. Winterberry tipped his hat down so that it covered his face.

Sprinkles snorted, blinked a few times, and closed his eyes.

Within a few seconds, both of them were snoring.

10

The Big Foot and Little Foot
Detective Agency

"But Boone," Hugo said as they walked along, "there's no such thing as the Big Foot and Little Foot Detective Agency."

"Sure there is! We just opened for business today. And if we find the treasure, Mr. Winterberry will give us half. That means we'll be able to buy the Marvelous Monster Magnet for sure."

"But we don't know how to find treasure," Hugo said.

"That's just because we've never tried. My grandma says that if you don't know where to start, you should just take small steps in the right direction. So, step one . . ." Boone unfolded the note that Mr. Winterberry had given them. It was a list that read:

1. GO TO THE PLACE NEAR THE SHARK'S TOOTH, WHERE SQUIDGES LOOK FOR THE GREMLIN'S SHOES.

2. CLIMB THE STAIRS TO NOWHERE.

3. PAT THE GIANT RATTLESNAKE.

Boone frowned. "Hmm. *Go to the place near the shark's tooth, where squidges look for the gremlin's shoes.* That's our first puzzle." He stopped walking and closed his eyes.

"What are you doing?" Hugo asked.

Boone opened his eyes again. "Waiting for a frog-in-a-bucket."

"What's that?"

"If you think hard enough about a problem," Boone ex-plained, "a good idea will start hopping around like crazy in your brain, just like a frog in a bucket. Doesn't that happen to you, too?"

Hugo shook his head. "I think I just get the regular sorts of ideas. The ones that don't hop."

"Oh. Well, maybe Sasquatches don't get frog-in-a-bucket ideas."

Hugo added a third item to his list of Reasons Why It Would Be Fun to Be a Human:

1. sneakers

2. pockets

3. frog-in-a-bucket ideas

Boone closed his eyes again and said, "Right now, I'm thinking about the problem of the gremlin's shoes."

Hugo watched Boone for another moment and then said, "Boone?"

"One sec."

"But Boone, I *know* where squidges go to look for the gremlin's shoes."

Boone's eyes flew open. "You do?"

"Sure. It's a game squidges play. You go to the top of a very steep hill, and you somersault down. If you go fast enough, you're supposed to find a little pair of gremlin shoes at the bottom of the hill. Then a gremlin appears and gives you a wish in exchange for the shoes. Gremlins love shoes."

"And pranks," Boone said knowingly. "There's a whole chapter on gremlins in *The Biggest Ever Book of Cryptids*. So, did you ever find a gremlin's shoes?"

"No. I probably didn't somersault fast enough. Plus, the hill near Widdershins

Cavern isn't very steep, so you just sort of flop down the hill instead of somersaulting."

"Oh. But you solved the first clue, Hugo!"

Hugo smiled. He'd never done detective work before. Maybe he was good at it.

"Now all we have to do is find a good hill to somersault down," Boone said. "It has to be tall and steep."

"But not too steep."

"And it should be grassy. Rocks would hurt."

"And there should be no trees that would get in the way of a good somersault." But then Hugo frowned. "What about the shark's tooth, though? The clue said to go

to the place near the shark's tooth. There aren't any sharks in the North Woods."

They were quiet for a moment, considering this problem. Boone closed his eyes, and Hugo waited for Boone to think about the shark's tooth. He hoped it wouldn't take too long. They had to deliver the package before it grew dark.

After a moment, Boone's eyes opened.

"I just had a frog-in-a-bucket!" he cried.

"Really? What is it?"

"I know a place in the North Woods where there's a tall, steep hill that is perfect for somersaulting," Boone told him. "It's right next to a large boulder, and that boulder is shaped just like a shark's tooth!"

"That must be it!" Hugo said. Then he frowned. "But what about the Stairs to Nowhere? And the giant rattlesnake?"

To be honest, that part of the treasure hunt worried him.

"One step at a time, Detective Hugo," Boone reminded him. "One step at a time."

11

Gremlin Hill

As they walked along, they talked about what the hidden treasure might be. Boone thought it was a pile of rubies, and Hugo thought it might be loads of nubbins or maybe a hundred jars of acorn butter.

Boone stopped walking suddenly. "Here we are." He pointed to a large boulder that was shaped like a shark's tooth. Beside the boulder was a hill that sloped down to a clearing below. The hill was tall and steep, but not too steep. It was soft and grassy, and there were no trees.

"What do you think?" Boone asked. "Would that be a good hill to somersault down for gremlin shoes?"

Hugo stared at the hill. His eyes grew wide. He could barely contain his excitement.

Here's the thing about Sasquatches: they LOVE to somersault! And a hill like this one, which was tall and steep, but not too steep, and also soft and grassy, was the perfect somersaulting hill!

"Um, sure. That looks like it might be

okay," Hugo replied. He spoke very calmly. Because here's the other thing about Sasquatches: even though they LOVE to somersault, they are also a little embarrassed about how much they love it.

"Then we've found our first clue!" Boone said.

"But, um . . . just to be sure, I think we should try it out," Hugo suggested shyly.

"You mean we should somersault down the hill?" Boone asked.

Hugo nodded, biting his lip to keep from smiling.

"Good idea," Boone said, leaving the package from Uncle Figgy's Toy Store beside the boulder. "I bet we'll go so fast that

we'll find gremlin shoes. If we do, what should we wish for?"

Hugo and Boone looked at each other, and at the same time, they both cried out, "A Marvelous Monster Magnet!"

"Ready?" said Boone.

"Set," said Hugo.

"GO!!!"

12

The Disaster

It was the best somersaulting Hugo had ever done! He tumbled so fast that it felt like he was a ball flying through the air. He laughed the whole way down, and when he reached the bottom of the hill, he lay flat on his back, still laughing. A moment later, Boone landed at the bottom of the hill beside him, also laughing.

When they had caught their breath, they sat up and looked around.

No gremlin shoes.

Hugo jumped to his feet. "Let's try again."

They scrambled back up the hill and somersaulted down again, then twice more, because they were sure they could go even faster.

After their fourth somersault down the hill—still no gremlin shoes—Hugo said,

"I'm beginning to think that somersaulting for gremlin shoes might be made up."

"Well, I have read all about gremlins," Boone admitted, "and I've never read anything about somersaulting for their shoes."

"It *is* a fun game, though," Hugo said. He was just about to suggest another somersault when Boone reminded him that they still had the treasure to find and the package to deliver before it got dark.

Hugo sighed. He could have somersaulted down that hill a dozen more times. Still, he knew Boone was right.

They headed back up the hill, but when they reached the boulder, they found that the package was gone.

"I left it right here," Boone insisted,

pointing to the spot beside the boulder. "I know I did!"

They searched all around the boulder, but the package had completely vanished.

"Uncle Figgy is going to be really mad at us," said Hugo.

"He'll want us to give him back the nubbins he paid us," Boone said.

"Which we don't have anymore," said Hugo miserably.

"And we'll probably have to pay for whatever was in that package. So unless we find Mr. Winterberry's treasure, we're in big trouble."

"How could the package just disappear?" Hugo asked. "Someone must have taken it. I didn't see anyone, did you?"

Boone shook his head.

But then Hugo thought of something.

"Maybe a gremlin stole the package?" he said.

"Hmm." Boone considered this possibility. "Gremlins *are* mischievous. And they're very small. The gremlin could have snuck through the high grass."

Hugo nodded. "And then dragged the package into the woods." He looked around. There were woods in every direction. "Which means the gremlin could be anywhere," he said in dismay.

Boone closed his eyes. He stood that way for a moment before he opened them again and smiled widely at Hugo.

"Did you just have another frog-in-a-bucket?" Hugo asked him.

Boone nodded excitedly.

"So? How will we find the gremlin?" Hugo asked.

"We don't have to find the gremlin," Boone replied. "The gremlin will come to us."

13

Gremlin Shoes

Boone sat down on the grass and began untying the laces on his sneakers.

"What are you doing?" Hugo asked him.

"Gremlins love shoes, right?"

Hugo nodded.

"So I'm trading my shoes for the package," Boone explained.

"But those are your new shoes!" Hugo cried. If he had a pair of new red sneakers with black stripes and yellow laces, he wasn't sure he'd be willing to trade them.

"I don't see how else we're going get the package back," Boone said determinedly. He took off his sneakers and placed them beside the boulder.

"Now what?" asked Hugo.

"Now we wait," Boone said.

They waited there for a few minutes, but nothing happened.

"Maybe we should wait at the bottom of the hill," Hugo said. "You know, in case the gremlin is afraid of being seen."

This made good sense.

And if we're being honest, Hugo was also hoping for one last somersault down the hill.

So they somersaulted down a fifth time. When they got to the bottom, they sat there, keeping very still, with their backs turned to the boulder to give the gremlin privacy. After a minute or so, they heard a shuffling sound from the top of the hill.

"Can you smell if that's the gremlin?" Boone whispered.

Hugo sniffed the air. He wasn't sure what a gremlin smelled like, but he *did* smell something. It was a mix of mushrooms and mud and an old campfire.

"It might be," Hugo whispered back.

They waited for as long as they could bear—which was only another minute or so. Then they jumped to their feet and ran up the hill to the boulder.

Boone's sneakers were gone. In their place was the package from Uncle Figgy's Toy Store.

Hugo picked up the package and shook it, just to make sure the toy was still inside. It thumped around in the box reassuringly. There was still a faint whiff of mushrooms

and mud and campfire in the air, but there was no sign of a gremlin.

"It worked!" Hugo cried.

When he turned to Boone, though, he saw that Boone was staring glumly at the spot where his sneakers had been.

"I guess I didn't think the gremlin would really take my sneakers," Boone said. "I mean, it's not like they'll fit. Gremlins are very small."

True, it had been Boone's idea to trade his sneakers for the package. But sometimes even frog-in-a-bucket ideas seem better in our brains than they do when they actually happen.

"Grandma's going to be mad," Boone said, almost to himself.

"We can try to trade again to get them back," said Hugo.

Boone thought for a minute. Then he

shook his head. "No. We were hired to deliver that package, and that's what we'd better do." He reached into his pocket and pulled out Mr. Winterberry's note again. "Number two says to climb the Stairs to Nowhere."

They looked all around.

"I don't see any stairs, do you?" Boone said.

"No, but there's an old path there." Hugo pointed to an overgrown path between two juniper trees. Then he looked down at Boone's feet. All he had on were socks. "Will you be okay walking?"

"Oh, sure!" Boone said, flapping his hand at Hugo. "My feet are as tough as a Sasquatch's!"

So they set off down the rough little path between the juniper trees, looking for the Stairs to Nowhere.

14

The Stairs to Nowhere

The path was so narrow that they had to walk single file. There were many tall old trees here, which blocked the sunlight and turned the woods dark and eerie. Hugo kept thinking about that giant rattlesnake that might be lurking underfoot, so he was looking down at the ground when Boone cried, "There it is!"

Hugo yelped and did a panicked hop.

"Where, where?" he asked, searching the ground for the sideways slither of the giant snake.

"There!" Boone pointed.

It wasn't the snake that Boone had spotted. It was a stone staircase. It had five steps, and at the top of the steps was . . . nothing at all.

The Stairs to Nowhere.

"We're supposed to climb them," Boone said.

That seemed weird. They were stairs to *nowhere*, after all. But they followed the note's directions and climbed the stairs anyway. When they got to the top step, they looked around.

There were piles of stones here and there, and something that looked like it had once been a fireplace.

"I bet there used to be a house here years and years ago," said Boone. "That's why the stairs are here."

"Maybe it burned down," Hugo said. "And maybe whoever lived here buried the treasure."

"Pirates bury treasure. Maybe they were pirates," Boone said. "Or bank robbers."

That was when Hugo spotted something off to his right. It was coiled up beneath a tree. Its body was as thick as Hugo's leg, and it wrapped around and around itself. Hugo guessed it would be as long as his whole classroom if it stretched itself out. The tip of its tail was raised in the air.

"*Snake.*" Hugo said the word as quietly as possible.

"What?" Boone just used his regular speaking voice, but to Hugo it sounded booming.

"*Shhh!*" Hugo pointed.

"Whoa!!" Boone cried when he saw the snake. "That thing is a monster!"

"*Shhh!*" Hugo warned him again. "What should we do?"

"Okay, um . . . okay . . . okay." Boone sounded nervous. Boone was hardly ever nervous, which made Hugo even more frightened. "Let's just stay very, very still and wait for it to leave."

15

The Giant Rattlesnake

Neither of them moved a muscle. They just stood on the top step of the Stairs to Nowhere and stared at the giant snake, waiting for it to slither away. They stood there for so long that Hugo began to worry they wouldn't be able to deliver the package before it grew dark.

Go away, go away! Hugo silently thought to the snake.

But the snake refused to budge.

There is something strange about that snake, Hugo thought. He sniffed the air suspiciously.

"Don't sniff so loudly," Boone whispered.

Hugo sniffed again.

"Wait here," Hugo said. He handed Boone the package and started walking toward the snake.

"Hugo, don't!" Boone cried.

Hugo picked up a thick branch that was lying on the ground. Slowly, he began to edge toward the snake. The snake kept perfectly still, staring at Hugo, its rattle poised in the air.

When Hugo was close enough, he lifted the stick. With one quick movement, he poked the snake with it.

"Are you crazy?!" Boone said.

But the snake didn't move.

Hugo reached out and tapped the snake's coiled body with the stick.

Tap-tap-tap.

It made a hollow sound.

Hugo turned around and smiled at Boone. "It's not a snake. It's just tree roots."

"Are you sure?" Boone asked.

Hugo went over to the snake and sat right on top of it. He grinned at Boone.

"Totally sure," he said, patting the "snake" on its head.

That was when Hugo saw the treasure chest.

16

Rubies and Nubbins

The treasure chest was tucked between the snaky tree roots, half covered with dirt. Hugo brushed away the dirt, and with a tug, he pulled the chest loose while Boone came over to join him.

"We did it!" Boone said. He hugged Hugo, who was holding the treasure chest—a carved wooden box with a handle.

They both jumped around and hooted, and the things in the treasure chest clinked and clattered.

"Should we open it?" Hugo asked when they stopped jumping.

"Mr. Winterberry didn't say not to."

But when they tried, they found that the chest was locked. There was a little keyhole in the lid, and though they looked all around the tree roots, there was no sign of a key.

Hugo shook the chest again to hear the clinking and clattering inside.

"It might be rubies," said Boone.

"Or nubbins," said Hugo.

"Or both."

"Definitely enough for a Marvelous Monster Magnet."

They took turns holding the treasure chest as they continued on to Green Hollow Cave, shaking it every so often for the fun of hearing what was inside.

The ground grew rockier, and a few times Boone had to sit down to rest his sore feet. It turned out his feet were not as tough as a Sasquatch's after all.

"I could carry you on my back," Hugo suggested.

"Nah, I'd be *way* too heavy for you," Boone said stoutly.

Hugo didn't think Boone would feel

heavy at all. In fact, Hugo was certain he'd carried bags of onions that were heavier than Boone. Still, Hugo didn't want to insult him, so he made sure to walk slowly instead so that Boone could keep up. And when Boone let out a little yelp because his socked foot had hit a sharp stone, Hugo pretended to sneeze at the same

time so that Boone would think he hadn't noticed.

Red sneakers with black stripes would be nice, Hugo thought, *but I think I'd rather have tough Sasquatch feet after all.*

He mentally scratched "sneakers" off his list of Reasons Why It Would Be Fun to Be a Human.

17

Green Hollow Cave

Green Hollow Cave was well hidden behind a waterfall that tumbled off the cliff above it and made a sound like a giant's sigh that never ended. You or I probably would have walked right by the waterfall and never noticed the cave. In fact, even though Boone had been to the waterfall many times and had swum in the little pool there, he had never even had an inkling that there was a cave behind it.

Hugo and Boone walked around the falls several times before they found a narrow ledge on which you could walk behind the falls. The ledge sloped upward and led

to a narrow cave entrance just big enough for them to squeeze inside.

"*Koooeee-koooooo!*" Hugo called into the darkness. That's the sound Sasquatches make whenever they enter another Sasquatch's cave. It's sort of like when a Human knocks on another Human's door.

After a moment, there was the sound of footsteps, and then Hugo and Boone saw a group of Sasquatches hurrying toward them down the passageway.

"Hello!" said Hugo happily, and waved.

The Sasquatches didn't wave back. They were too busy staring at Boone.

"Is that . . . IS THAT . . ." one of them asked in shock.

It was then that Hugo realized his mistake. Bringing a Human into a strange Sasquatch cave was the worst possible thing a Sasquatch could do.

"It's okay, he's a *friendly* Human," Hugo told them quickly.

But the Sasquatches didn't seem to hear him. Or else they didn't care. They walked right past Hugo and surrounded Boone.

"No! Wait, please!" cried Hugo. He tried to push past the crowd, but there were so many of them, and they were all much bigger than him. Finally, Hugo turned sideways and wedged himself between two of them, frantically trying to get to Boone, who was trapped in the circle of Sasquatches.

"Don't hurt him!" Hugo pleaded once he had managed to push into the middle of the circle. "He's my friend, his name is—"

"Oh, we know who he is!" one of the Sasquatches said with excitement in her voice. "He's famous in the North Woods!" She bowed deeply. "It's an honor to meet you, Boone."

18

Uncle Figgy's Special Delivery

It seemed that word had spread throughout the North Woods about a small Human boy who went to Sasquatch school and played with all the squidges in Widdershins Cavern.

More and more Sasquatches rushed down the passageway to greet them. Some Sasquatches were shy and hung back, staring. And of course, there were one or two who were not at all happy to see a Human in a Sasquatch cave. But most of the Sasquatches flocked around Boone, eager to meet a friendly Human.

"You're as famous as Mad Marvin!" Hugo whispered to Boone.

There was such a fuss that for a while Hugo and Boone forgot why they had come in the first place. It was Hugo who finally remembered. While one of the Sasquatches was examining Boone's hairless arm in wonder, Hugo nudged Boone.

"The package from Uncle Figgy's," Hugo reminded him.

"Right!" Boone said. "Um, excuse me," he said, holding up the box. "We actually came here to deliver a package from Uncle Figgy's Toy Store. It's for . . ." He checked the label. "It's for Lila Whisperwind."

"That's my daughter!" A Sasquatch with big bright eyes stepped forward. "If you two delivered it to her in person, she would be thrilled!"

So of course they couldn't refuse.

The crowd led Hugo and Boone through a tangle of passageways. They were much narrower than the ones in Widdershins Cavern. There were some spots where everyone had to walk sideways in order to fit through. This was tricky for Hugo since he was carrying the treasure chest, but he managed.

Green Hollow Cave wasn't nearly as big as Widdershins Cavern. There were no bakeries or toy stores. The walls were painted with cheerful murals of Sasquatches splashing in pools and playing games and having feasts. As they walked through the passageways, Hugo and Boone could hear the waterfall sighing loudly outside the cave.

The Sasquatches led Hugo and Boone into a small apartment. It was only one room, and not a very big one. Lying on a bed in the corner was a very small squidge. She looked like she had been lying there for quite a while. There were books scattered across her blankets and cups and plates by her bedside.

"Lila, do you know who this is?" her mother asked in an excited voice.

Lila scooched up to a sitting position. She stared at Boone. For a moment, she seemed too shocked to speak.

"It's Boone," she said in a voice that was thin and wispy but full of amazement.

"Hi, Lila." Boone smiled at her.

"You have polka dots on your face," Lila said to him.

"Oh, those are my freckles," said Boone. "I have thirty-eight of them. You can count them if you want to." Boone sat on the edge of Lila's bed so that Lila could count the freckles on his face. But she could only count up to ten, so she had to trust him that there were thirty-eight.

"Hugo and Boone brought a package for you," Lila's mother said, and handed Lila the box.

"What is it?" she asked.

"Open it and see."

Lila's fingers fumbled as she tried to open the box, so Mrs. Whisperwind helped her with it. She pulled a note out of the package and read it to Lila.

"'For Lila: this little fellow needed a home. Feel better! Love, Aunt Merry.'" Mrs. Whisperwind turned to Hugo and Boone and explained, "Lila's been sick for a while."

"But I'm better now," Lila said.

"Much better." Mrs. Whisperwind smiled. "Now, look and see what's inside."

Lila reached in and pulled out a stuffed toy. It was made of reddish-brown cloth and had a furry white chest and a white-tipped tail. It had shiny dark eyes made of smooth glass. On its head was a jaunty green cap, and it had green shoes on all four feet.

"A fox!" Lila squealed.

"It looks just like a real fox, doesn't it?" Mrs. Whisperwind said.

Lila held it up and looked at it. "Yes." She tilted her head to one side. "Except that foxes don't wear clothes."

"You can take them off. See?" Her mom showed her how the little hat and shoes came off. "What are you going to name it?"

Lila thought for a minute. "Boogo," she said. "For Boone and Hugo."

19

Frog-in-a-Bucket

After a quick lunch at Green Hollow Cave, Hugo and Boone started their journey back. They went slowly because of Boone's sore feet. They retraced their steps, patting the head of the giant rattlesnake and climbing down the Stairs to Nowhere. When they reached the shark's tooth boulder, Hugo stopped.

"Let's have one last somersault," he said.

"Okay," said Boone. "But what should we do with the treasure chest? The gremlin might steal it."

"Good point. Let's leave it at the bottom of the hill. That way we can keep an eye on it."

They set the treasure chest at the bottom of the hill, then walked back up to somersault.

Boone went first. He launched himself down the hill and somersaulted at top speed all the way to the bottom. Next came Hugo, laughing the whole way down.

"One more time!" Hugo said.

As they started back up the hill, Hugo hooked his thumbs together and held them up in the air.

"Why are you doing that with your thumbs?" Boone asked.

"It's what Sasquatches do when they are hoping something will happen."

"Oh! It's like when people cross their fingers!" said Boone.

"Then maybe you should cross your fingers."

"Okay." Boone crossed his fingers. "But why?"

"You'll see in a minute."

They climbed the hill, Hugo linking his thumbs in the air and Boone crossing his fingers.

116

When they reached the top, Hugo rushed over to the boulder and bent down. When he turned around, he was holding up a pair of red sneakers with black stripes and yellow laces.

"My sneakers!" Boone cried. "How did you get them back?"

"The idea came to me when Lila's mother took the shoes off the fox. I thought, *Hey, those little fox shoes would probably fit a gremlin perfectly! Maybe we could trade them for Boone's sneakers.* I got so excited about the idea that I could hardly sit still! At lunch, I asked Mrs. Whisperwind if I could have the fox shoes since Lila didn't want them. Then I put them by the boulder while you somersaulted down the hill, and . . . *ta-da!*"

"Hugo!"

"What?"

"You had a frog-in-a-bucket idea!" Boone said.

"Oh! Wow. I guess I did."

That was another thing Hugo could cross off his list of Reasons Why It Would Be Fun to Be a Human. Now the only thing on the list was "pockets."

After Boone put on his sneakers, he stood up, cupped his hands around his mouth, and shouted, "If you can hear me, Gremlin, I hope you like your new shoes!"

And from somewhere deep in the woods, they heard a peal of laughter.

20

The Treasure Chest

r. Winterberry and Sprinkles
were still snoring when Hugo
and Boone returned.

"Wake up, Mr. Winterberry." Hugo
spoke softly, so as not to startle him. "We
found your treasure chest."

Mr. Winterberry tipped up his hat and

opened his eyes. Sprinkles opened his eyes, too.

"You found it? Already? The Big Foot and Little Foot Detective Agency works fast."

"The only problem is that it's locked, and there's no key."

"That's no problem." Mr. Winterberry reached up to his hatband and pulled out a small wooden key. "This should do the trick," he said.

Hugo put the treasure chest down

in front of Mr. Winterberry, and he and Boone sat on the ground beside him. They watched intently as Mr. Winterberry put the key in the lock. Even Sprinkles seemed to be watching.

There was a little click as Mr. Winterberry turned the key.

"Ready?" he asked them with a glint in his eye.

Hugo and Boone nodded.

Slowly, Mr. Winterberry lifted the lid.

Hugo and Boone leaned forward to see what was inside.

There were no rubies.

There weren't any nubbins, either.

But there was pretty much everything else.

There was a carved dragon that flew high in the air when you pulled a string, a thick rope perfect for a tightrope, a toy raft made of sticks bound together, a little book of ghost stories with pictures, a wooden whistle, a ball made of willow branches, three perfect arrowheads, and many other fascinating things.

After Hugo, Boone, and Mr. Winterberry had carefully examined all the items, Mr. Winterberry shook his head and sighed.

"Ahhh, this brings back memories," he said in a dreamy way.

"What do you mean?" Hugo asked.

"All of this was mine. Well, mine and Sam's. He was my best friend when we lived in the North Woods many years ago. We spent all our time together, playing games, having adventures. But one day, a Human discovered our cavern, so of course all of us Sasquatches had to leave in a hurry. Before our families left, Sam and I put all our special treasures in a box and hid it. Then we wrote out the directions for finding it again when we moved back to the North Woods so we wouldn't forget."

"But you didn't move back?" Boone asked.

Mr. Winterberry shook his head. "My family went south, and Sam's family went west, and after a while we lost touch. But this year, I felt like it was time to see my old home again. And to find our old treasure chest." He looked at Hugo and Boone. "Now, I know I told you I'd split the treasure with you two, but I've changed my mind." He shut the chest with a hard *thunk*. "I don't want to split it." He pushed the chest toward them. "I want you to have it all."

"But then you came all this way for nothing," Hugo said.

"Nothing?! Pah! Sprinkles and I have had many adventures on our trip. That's the best part of life, isn't it? Having adventures. Oh, and one more thing . . ." Mr.

Winterberry reached up and took off his hat. Balanced on his head was a small red pouch. He opened it, counted out some coins, and handed them to Boone. "That's twenty-five nubbins, enough for your Marvelous Monster Magnet."

For a moment, Hugo and Boone didn't even know what to say. But when they began to thank him, Mr. Winterberry waved it away. "Consider it a tip for all your good detective work. Now"—he stood up and patted Sprinkles's back—"hop on! You two can ride Sprinkles back home, and then you'll see that a moose is better than a boat any day."

21

Moose versus Boat

In some ways, riding a moose was not that different from riding in a boat on choppy water. Hugo and Boone swayed from side to side and rocked backward and forward. Once or twice, Sprinkles went into a fast trot, which felt like sailing on a strong river current. But then Sprinkles would spy

an acorn or a tree bud and would stop to nibble on it.

"Just think," said Boone as they rode along. Mr. Winterberry was walking ahead of them, carrying the treasure chest. "We can go straight to Uncle Figgy's Toy Store when we get back and buy a Marvelous Monster Magnet just like that. *Blammo!*" Boone snapped his fingers.

"And then we won't even have to go

searching for cryptids anymore," Hugo said. "We'll just blow into the Marvelous Monster Magnet, and the cryptids will come to us."

They were silent for a minute.

Then Boone said, "Which, if you think about it, wouldn't be as much fun as searching for them."

"Some of our best adventures have been searching for cryptids. Remember the Tommyknocker?"

"And don't forget the Ripple Worms!" said Boone.

They were silent for the rest of the trip.

The great thing about best friends is that they don't always need to say things out loud in order to understand each other perfectly.

When they reached Widdershins Cavern, Mr. Winterberry put down the treasure chest and helped them off Sprinkles.

"So, what do you think? Moose or boat?" asked Mr. Winterberry.

"It's close, but I'm sticking with boats," Boone said. He patted the moose. "No offense, Sprinkles, but boats don't stop and eat acorns every few minutes."

Boone took the twenty-five nubbins out

of his pocket and handed them back to Mr. Winterberry. "Thanks so much for the nubbins," he said, "but Hugo and I have decided that we don't want a Marvelous Monster Magnet after all."

"It would take the excitement out of looking for the monsters ourselves," Hugo said.

"Ahh." Mr. Winterberry nodded. "Very wise. Sam and I would have felt exactly the same way. Well, you two have certainly changed my mind about Sasquatches being friends with Humans . . . even if I haven't changed *your* minds about boats." He pulled the treasure chest key from his hatband and held it out to Hugo. "Keep this safe."

"You should probably give it to Boone," Hugo said. "He's got pockets."

"A Sasquatch doesn't need pockets," Mr. Winterberry said. "He just needs a good hat." He took off his hat and put it on Hugo's head. "This one is yours now." He tucked the key to the treasure chest back into the hatband.

"But Mr. Winterberry, I can't take your hat," Hugo objected.

"Nonsense! I have other hats at home. Anyway, that's my special adventuring hat, and you, my young friend, are a born adventurer."

"Wow," said Hugo, adjusting the hat. "Thank you!"

"Pockets" was the last item on Hugo's list of Reasons Why It Would Be Fun to Be a Human. Now he mentally scratched that off the list, too.

Mr. Winterberry hopped up on Sprinkles's back and tied his red pouch to Sprinkles's antler.

"So long, Detectives Hugo and Boone! Here's to many more adventures for all of us!" And with a quick pat on Sprinkles's shoulder, they trotted off, back into the deep woods.

The sky was growing dark now. Sasquatches call this time of day "the dimmery." All over the North Woods, Humans were snug in their homes, eating their suppers and getting ready for bed. But the dimmery was when Sasquatches came out to play. Outside Widdershins Cavern, Sasquatch families were setting up picnic dinners, and squidges were chasing each other. Hugo's classmates were all there: Malcolm and Izzy were playing the Ha-Ha Game, and Gigi and Pip were leaping over each other, playing Jimminy-Jimminy-Jump. Even grumpy Roderick was tapping his feet to the music from Mrs. Nukluk's fiddle while grown-up Sasquatches danced and laughed and spun each other around.

"Sasquatches really know how to have

fun," said Boone dreamily. "Sometimes I wish I were a squidge."

"You do?" Hugo said, surprised. "That's funny, because sometimes I wish I were a Human."

"Really?"

Hugo nodded.

They were quiet for a moment as they watched some of the little squidges somersault down a short hill, flopping and laughing.

"But maybe we're fine being just who we are," Hugo said finally.

"Yeah, Big Foot and Little Foot," said Boone.

"Exactly."

"Hey, Big Foot?"

"What?" Hugo asked.

"Feel like somersaulting?"

Hugo smiled. "I always feel like somer-saulting, Little Foot."

They joined the little squidges on the hill, tumbling and flopping and laughing the whole way down as the sun set in the deep North Woods.

ACKNOWLEDGMENTS

Sasquatches know that we all need help if we want to do things right, and that's why I want to thank my wonderful "Sasquatch Community." Major thanks to my editor, Erica Finkel, for her clear-sighted wisdom. I am forever grateful to my agent, Alice Tasman, who is even better than thirty jars of acorn butter. Thanks to Felicita Sala for bringing Hugo and his friends to life with her beautiful illustrations. Big thanks to the entire Abrams team for spreading the word about Hugo and Boone. And finally, as always, thanks to my practically perfect husband, Adam, and my own squidge, Ian.